The Miracle of Ramadan

By Wassim Hijazi

LANTERN PUBLICATIONS

Lantern Publications
info@lanternpublications.com
www.lanternkids.com.au

A catalogue record for this book is available from the National Library of Australia

Ordering Information:
Quantity sales. Special discounts are available on quantity purchases by corporations, associations, and others. For details, contact the distributor at the address above.

Acknowledgements: Richard McRoberts and Sis Julie Karaki for their invaluable editing skills
Artwork: Leyla Teymoorinejhad

All characters depicted in this story are fictitious. Any resemblance to actual people or places is purely coincidental.

ISBN - 978-1-922583-25-3 pbk
ISBN - 978-1-922583-27-7 hbk

First Edition

In the Name of God,
the Most Compassionate, the Most Merciful

In loving memory of Haji Mariam Jebeile Hijazi

"Al Fatiha"

The month of Ramadan is a time of faith, a time to ask God for forgiveness and help. It is a time when families and friends break bread together. It is a time when destiny is written. And it is a time when miracles take place.

Let me tell you a story. This is a story of a man who had lost his way. A man who needed to learn to love again.

Many years ago, at the month of Ramadan, a miracle happened that changed all our lives forever.

Let me take you back ...

Mansour's Ghost

Long ago, in a faraway land, lived a man called Karim Malik. Karim was a very important man in the village.

Al Tawbah had once been a place of peace and plenty. But then came the war. The soldiers had come, with their guns and their bombs. The militias fought one another. There had been battles in the streets. Terrible things happened. Many people had been killed, on both sides. Fathers died. Brothers died. A great many women died. Children were orphaned every day. Blood was spilt … so much blood.

Many of the houses were destroyed. There were ruins everywhere. Most of the shops had been blown up. Homeless children wandered the streets begging for food.

In summer there was not enough to eat, and water was scarce. In winter, it was bitterly cold.

The only thing keeping the town going was a factory. The Malik factory had avoided the worst of the war. It was owned by Karim. It made shoes – excellent shoes – affordable shoes. Because of their reputation, the Malik brand was known throughout the country. As a result, Malik was a wealthy man, a very wealthy man. Since the factory was for most people of Al Tawbah the only work available, there was just enough work for the people.

It sounds like this is going to be a happy story. I wish that were true. Alas, it should be. But for one thing. Karim Malik was a very successful businessman. He worked hard. He counted his money, down to the last penny. He was careful in everything he did.

But did people love him for it? No. Why? Because as a human being, he was cold, and bitter, and greedy. Karim was *not* a generous man. He was not a kind man. He was – there is no other word for it - a miser.

On the evening our story starts, it is the last day of Ramadan, the evening before Eid. Let us visit the Malik factory.

In the glow of the gas lamps, all the workers were busy making shoes. The cutters had brought the leather in from the leather room. The closers were busy taking the pieces of leather and sewing them together. The finishers were stitching the uppers onto the soles. Everyone was busy.

In charge of the factory – the foreman – was Rami. He was walking up and down the benches and watching everyone, with the eye of an eagle.

"Faster!" he called out. "There are orders for all these shoes. Stop talking. Get on with it."

"But sir," said one woman. "Please. We're working as hard as we can."

"Silence! I will decide how hard you work. Do you want a job or not?"

He glared at her.

Everyone looked down. Rami was not someone to be crossed. He was Mr. Malik's right-hand man, and he was known for his iron will.

At that moment Mr. Malik arrived.

Most of the workers were wearing the traditional thawb. Not Mr. Malik. He was tall and thin. Once he had been handsome, but now he was pale and irritable. He was wearing a black suit and tie. He opened the door, and looked in.

He walked down the aisle.

"Salaam," he said in a loud voice.

Everyone responded in a whisper, "Salaam."

One of the workers was a man named Ali. As Malik passed where Ali was working on the last of a shoe, he said, "Salaam." Ali looked into Malik's eyes hopefully and smiled.

Malik looked away. He flicked his cuffs, tightened his tie and kept going. He was due to have a meeting with Rami. They would discuss supplies and orders, and how to ship the shoes to the big city in time for spring.

Rami followed him into the board room. It was a grand room, all in rich wood panelling, with beautiful gas fittings for light. There was a long wooden table of oak. On the wall were framed photographs of their most popular shoes. And charts showing the sales they have made to their various customers.

The two men sat at the end of the table.

A woman came into the room. She was carrying a tray with two glasses of sweet tea, and almond biscuits. She set these down on the table in front of the boss bowing slightly.

Mr Malik looked up from his papers and saw her. His face flushed. He turned back to his figures.

"Thank you," he said sharply. "Please leave them. We are busy."

"Thank you, Mariam," said Rami.

She went, silently.

The year had been going well for the Malik factory. They were swamped with orders. Business had never been better.

"Aren't you pleased?" said Rami. "This is our best sales period ever!" said Rami pointing to the figures.

"Hmmph. They're good enough, I suppose. But this year we can top them. I'm sure you'll agree."

"Yes sir."

"Are the workers doing enough? You need to watch them, you know. They'll take advantage if you give them the chance."

"Yes, sir."

At this point, there was a knock on the door.

"Come!" said Rami.

The door opened. It was Ali.

"Yes?"

"I apologise, sir. But could I have a word?"

Malik motioned him into the room.

Ali walked into the room with a limp. His leg had been permanently injured in the war. There was pain with every step he took. Ali Akeel had been a famous general in the war. Some of the battles he had led had become folklore.

But now…. like many in Al Tawbah, he had no other option than to work in the factory.

"We're listening." said Karim.

"Sir, you know what day it is tomorrow…"

"Of course, I know. So?"

"We were wondering if you would permit us to have the day off?"

"What? A day off? Are you joking?"

"But sir, Eid is …"

"Just another day for work. Another day to make money. Rami – you see what I mean? They will take advantage if you give them the chance."

"Sir, all we want is the time to go to the mosque. So, we can pray and spend the holy day celebrating with family and friends. Please, sir."

"How dare you! There is no way I will be letting my workers off. Think of the money I will lose. Do I pay you to stay away from work? Do I?"

"No sir. But it is Eid. It is a holy time. I beg you …"

I regret to say that, at this, Malik laughed out loud and continued to tease Ali.

"I tell you what," he said, "you can take the Sunday off."

"But sir, that's our normal day of rest."

"Exactly. You can wait."

I wish I could tell you that Mr. Malik felt guilty at this. But his heart was cold.

"Off you go. And don't interrupt again if you want to keep your job!"

Out in the factory, Ali reported the grim news: the boss would not be closing the factory for Eid.

"There's too much work. Mr. Malik has no other option but to stay open tomorrow. The orders that we have coming in from the big city are simply too much. We won't make the shoes in time if we close tomorrow." Ali explained to the workers

They would all be required to come in the next day.

The workers' disappointment showed on their faces. But they had not expected anything else. They had become used to Ali making excuses for Mr. Malik and easing tensions between the workers and management in the factory. In the factory, just as in the war, Ali was known for his leadership and people skills. So much so that he was known as "The General" in the factory.

By that time, the sun was about to set. The end of the working day had come. The workers filed out of the factory and made their way home.

Now it was the time for the feast to celebrate the breaking of the fast.

In a hall nearby, one of the few in Al Tawbah that had survived the war, the workers and their families had set up the feast. The wooden tables were covered with food of all kinds. There were big dishes of kibbeh, kafta and manakish, with lentil soup, fatoush and tabouleh.

There were big urns of water, to fill the glasses with sweet tea. There were plates of delicious maamoul and shaabiyat and baklava. The wives had been busy. Despite the shortages, they had found enough to make a wonderful feast for the breaking of the last fast of the Month of Ramadan, the night before Eid.

The families prayed together. They were asking for forgiveness and pledging their faith.

And because of the hard lives they had lived since the war, someone quoted a verse of the Quran,

"With every hardship there is ease!" (94:6)

Meanwhile, back at the factory, Malik and his foreman had finished their meeting.

"We must all try harder," said Malik with a frown. "Don't think life is easy. It's not! We need the money, and it is up to us to bring it in."

"Yes, sir." said Rami. "Now that it is Eid, do you think we should donate a little to Hajj Fawzi, the kind man who helps the poor? There are so many orphans, and he is feeding them. We are making a lot of money. What do you think?"

"Don't be stupid! I've given enough to him over the years. And I pay enough taxes to this corrupt government. Why should I care? We don't need religion. We don't need to give away anything. We need to build the business and save up for more machines so we can produce even more shoes. And make more money…"

"Yes sir. Happy Eid, sir."

'Hmph," muttered Malik. "All right then, be off with you."

Rami bowed and left.

Alone, Malik walked through the factory. He checked to see that all the machines had been turned off, and all the gas lamps extinguished. You can't be too careful, he said to himself. People are careless. They don't deserve my generosity.

Finally, he went to the big front door, and stepped outside.

He turned the key in the lock.

He looked at the sign above the building.

"Mansour and Malik," it said, in grand letters.

He thought of Mansour for the first time in ages. Mansour was now seven years dead. His old business partner had been the reason Karim had got into the shoe trade in the first place. Mansour was from a rich family. He understood business. Before the war, they had started the factory together. It was then called "Mansour and Malik Shoes." Mansour had promised Karim success, if he just took the risk.

Mansour had been right. Malik had taken the risk, invested his money, worked hard – and now he was successful. He was a rich man. A very rich man.

He looked at the sign and brooded.

What would his old friend think now? He would be pleased, surely. Malik had taken the business to new heights. He was now rich beyond what Mansour had promised.

Then why did he feel so sad?

Malik turned and walked down the streets, on his way home. It was silent. A cold winter night. The new moon was born, and it was in its crescent, shining beautifully high up in the black sky.

The streets of the town were still covered with rubble from where the bombs had exploded. He had to walk around the bricks and piles of dust.

Halfway down the street, there was a child, begging.

"Please," said the child, "could you spare a penny?"

Malik looked straight ahead, pretending he didn't see the child.

He walked on as fast as he could.

Suddenly, he heard the sound of the call to prayer. It was drifting through the town, from the minaret at the mosque.

"Oh no, not that," said Malik, covering his ears. He didn't want to be reminded that he no longer prayed. He knew that he had turned away from God. Did he feel guilty? Of course not, he said to himself.

He hurried on.

In the main square, as he passed, he saw lights on in the hall. The door was open, and the sound of laughter came out.

"What's that ridiculous noise?" He wondered.

He went closer. He looked inside.

The hall was golden with light. The families were sitting around, talking, and sharing food. His workers. He recognised them all.

He stepped into the hall.

They were all having a wonderful time. Families and friends. Adults and children. All celebrating the breaking of the fast.

Malik stood near the door, peering in.

And then, someone turned.

It was Mariam. She looked up at him.

Her eyes filled with tears.

"Here we go again," muttered Malik. He frowned and hurried out into the night.

At the best end of town was his house. It was a magnificent building. He had bought it in the early days of his success. The owner, once a great man, had fallen on hard times. Malik had got it for a song. Some had accused him of taking advantage, but for him it was simply a great bargain. Why should he care?

He unlocked the door and hung up his coat. He went to the kitchen. His housekeeper had left him some supper – hummus and flat bread as well as a glass of water.

He ate it quickly.

Then he went up to his bedroom. It was a big house, but most of the rooms were empty. There was no heating. It was freezing cold.

In his bedroom, he locked the door. Can't be too careful, he thought. He took off his suit and put it neatly on the dresser. Then he put on a dressing gown and a woolen cap – for it was icy cold - and climbed into bed. He lit a candle which he placed on the bedside table.

Outside the window, he could see the newly born moon, high in the night sky.

Of course … the Month of Ramadan, he thought. They're all going crazy. Who cares? They don't know the meaning of life. You're born, you work, you die. That's all there is.

He laid back onto the pillow and dozed.

Suddenly, he heard a voice.

"Salaam Alykum Karim."

Malik looked up.

He couldn't believe what he saw.

It was Mansour. His old friend and business partner.

Mansour was sitting on the chair at the foot of the bed, looking straight at him.

"What? Who? Get away!"

Malik gathered the blankets around him and pulled away.

"It's me, Mansour. Your friend."

"But you can't be here!" cried Malik. "You're dead. Dead for seven years!"

"Perhaps. But listen - I have come to you with something that you need."

"I don't need anything!" growled Malik.

"Are you happy?" said the ghost.

"Of course. Perfectly happy."

"Then why are you alone? Why have you no wife or children? Why are you here when you could be with all the others, celebrating Eid?"

"All that is nonsense," said Malik. "What do I need with religion? I have my business. I have my money. Mansour, do you know how much I have made?"

"I do. And did it bring you happiness?"

Malik was silent.

"What of Mariam?" said the ghost.

"What of her?"

"She is sad. And so, she should be."

"That is her affair," said Malik sharply.

"And Ali?"

"He is a fool," said Malik. "He is lucky that he has a job at all."

"Karim, I tell you that you need to learn a lesson."

"Lesson?"

"Like you, I thought only of money. I thought that was what I was put on Earth for. To become a rich man.

How foolish I was. I did not know that death would claim me when I was a young man. I did not know how little time I had."

"But business was what we did. That was what mattered."

"Karim, our real business is life. It is people. It is things we – you and I - had forgotten God, mercy, charity, and love."

"Mansour, what's the matter with you? Have you gone mad?"

"No. I have seen the light."

And Mansour pointed out the window. The newly born moon hung there in the sky.

"I have seen what I did wrong. And I have repented."

"What has this to do with me?" asked Karim

"Karim, you will have some visitors tonight."

"Visitors? What sort?"

"Angels."

"That's ridiculous. I don't believe in angels. I barely even believe in God." He pulled his cap down over his face. "I don't want to see anyone."

"Don't turn your back on God, he is always with you."

"Turn my back on God? HE IS THE ONE WHO TURNED HIS BACK ON ME!" snapped Karim

Mansour shook his head and was disappointed in his old friend's reaction.

"You will have the chance now to see what you have become. And I hope that you take this last chance."

"What last chance?"

"Before you die."

Malik clutched his blanket around him.

"Die?"

"Make the most of your life," said Mansour. "Find God again and make the right choices this time, you don't get a second chance at life my friend. "

And with that, Mansour rose.

He went to the door.

And passed right through it.

"Mansour, come back! Please ..."

Malik was now completely alone.

"Foolishness!"

"Madness!"

"Last chance indeed!"

He picked up a book of accounts and started to go through them.

But his heart was not in the work.

"Bah!" he said. "I'm perfectly happy as I am."

He lay back. And fell fast asleep.

The First Angel

he clock struck one.

Karim woke startled.

He sat up. What foolishness, he thought to himself. What an idiot I am. To think that Mansour had come back from the dead.

Did I talk to him? Was it all a dream? Of course, it was.

But then he began to think about what his dream visitor had said.

"Our real business is life… I have repented…This is your last chance – before you die."

Karim clutched his gown around him. A sudden fear gripped him.

What if he died young, like Mansour? No one had expected Mansour to die in his mid-twenties. He had been fit, healthy, and rich.

But coming back from the big city after one visit, he had fallen ill. It was a fever of some kind, no one knew what.

His parents had summoned the best doctors. When he didn't get better, they called in a specialist from the capital. No expense was spared. They gave him the best medicines. Yet Mansour got weaker and weaker. And finally…

Karim remembered following his coffin through the streets of Al Tawbah to the cemetery. Like Mansour's parents and older brother, Karim was dressed in black. He remembered,

"We created you from it, and return you into it, and from it we raise you a second time." (Quran 20:55)

Karim was the last to throw the dirt into the grave and farewell his old friend.

Can death come so quickly?

What if I should die now too?

He got up out of bed and walked nervously up and down.

Only God knows.

What am I saying? He no longer prayed. He had turned his back on God. But he remembered these words:

"And fear the day when ye shall be brought back to God. Then shall every soul be paid what it earned, and none shall be dealt with unjustly." (Quran 2:281)

What had he earned? Plenty of money, yes, but what else? Had he been charitable? Or merciful? Or good?

Despite the cold, Karim began to sweat. Mansour's words had shaken him.

He went to the window. The crescent moon was hanging high in the sky.

Karim stared at it. How had he come to this? How had he changed so much?

Then he saw something. A bright light was directly above the moon. It was white and dazzling, like a star. And it was getting bigger.

Karim rubbed his eyes. He shook his head. And he looked again.

The bright light was growing bigger with every second that passed.

Karim retreated inside his room. Maybe this was another dream?

The light was now shining right into his house. He could make out every detail of his bed, the table with its candle, the chair, the mirror on the wall, his wardrobe.

Something was coming – as Mansour had said.

Karim scrambled back into bed. He climbed in and pulled the covers over him.

The room was now brilliant with light.

Karim closed his eyes again and held his breath.

"KARIM," said a deep voice. "KARIM."

He opened his eyes.

A figure stood before him. It glowed like a heavenly vision. It was like a man. Except that it had a glowing face, almost too difficult to look at directly. It was wearing long flowing robes of green. And it was looking down at him.

"Yes?" said Karim, trembling.

"Karim, I have come for you."

"On no," said Karim, pulling away to the back of the bed. "Are you the angel of death?"

"No. He will visit you later."

"Then who are you?"

"I am the Angel of Ramadan of the Past. I have come to show you how you once were."

"Please, Angel. I have done nothing wrong. Please…"

And Karim shrunk away.

"You had every chance," said the angel. "But did you make the most of it?"

"I tried my best," said Karim. "I tried to be good."

"Karim, we are going to go back in time now. We are going to revisit your past. And learn some lessons."

"Must I?" said Karim, cowering in his bed.

"Yes. You need to come with me," said the angel.

And with that, he reached out his hand.

Karim felt himself lifted up.

The angel took Karim.

And made for the window.

"But Angel, I am a mortal. I will fall. Please."

"Take my hand. You are completely safe."

"Where are we going?"

"Into the past."

And with that, they went out through the window into the night sky.

Karim found himself high up in the air, looking down on the village.

And yet, it was not the village as he knew it.

There were no broken buildings, or shattered walls.

It was Al Tawbah. But it was perfect in every way. It was as if there had never been a war.

Then Karim realised: it was the village of his childhood.

The angel descended slowly and gracefully from the night sky. They alighted in the main square. And made their way towards a house in a side street.

It was Karim's house. Not the magnificent house he had bought with his wealth. The humble house of his childhood.

They moved through the wall like ghosts. They were looking at the kitchen. Sitting there were four people.

Karim's eyes filled with tears. It was his first Month of Ramadan fasting. He was eight years old.

There were his father and mother, and his beloved twin sister, Zahra. And a little boy. It was Karim as a child.

They were all sitting around the table in the kitchen. The sun had set, so they had broken their fast. On the table were the remains of the meal.

Now his mother brought out dishes of ma'amoul and kaa'k. Karim watched as the children reached out and took the sweets that he loved so much. Everyone laughed. His father reached out and ruffled his hair. His mother smiled at her husband and her two children. It was a scene of love and happiness.

Now something special. His father opened a bag and handed it over to his mother. She opened it and a wonderful smile came over her face. It was a hijab in green – a silk scarf.

"Were your family wealthy?" asked the angel.

"No. My father would have saved for months to get that gift. We had just enough to survive, but we were always happy," said Karim with a warm smile.

Now the mother handed her husband a small box. His father opened it. Inside was a beautiful tasbih. He smiled. Then reached over and kissed her on the forehead.

Now the father took a box from under the table. He beckoned to young Karim. The boy approached. He handed the box to the boy. Inside were a pair of shiny new leather shoes – ideal for going to the mosque and school.

The boy embraced his father warmly. Was this one of the reasons that Karim had wanted to open a shoe factory?

And finally, the mother handed Zahra a parcel wrapped in paper. The girl opened it. Inside was a new sky-blue abaya. She leapt up and hugged her mother.

It was a scene of such beauty that Karim put his hands over his face. There was a pain in his heart which he couldn't explain.

"What do you see?" said the angel.

"I see my family – when I was a boy."

"What do you see in your heart?"

"I see a scene of love."

"Go on."

"I see kindness and compassion."

"And what about you – when you were a boy?" asked the angel.

Karim choked back a tear, and said,

"I see a boy who loved others…"

"Indeed," said the angel. "And is that the Karim I fetched from his grand house tonight?"

"No … No. It is not. But I was just a child there, full of hope. It's different now," said Karim defensively. "I run a big factory. I have so much on my plate. The world isn't the same. I adapted. It's a tough world we live in now".

This is where he had started. With his loving parents and his wonderful sister.

"Come," said the angel. "We have other things to see."

And so saying, the angel took him by the hand and they rose into the air.

The village looked wonderful in the golden moonlight.

Karim felt a great sense of calm.

He no longer wished to be back in his bed. Or in his factory. He realised he was pleased to be visiting his past.

The angel swooped down again, and they landed outside a big building.

"My school," said Karim. "But it was bombed in the war. It no longer exists."

"Ah," said the angel, "but in your past it does. Let us go in."

And with that, they moved through the tall wall and into the courtyard.

It was as bright as day. There were children everywhere, running around and laughing happily.

"My friends," said Karim. He smiled with pleasure.

"Tell me who they are."

"Why, there is Zahra, my twin sister." Then he pointed to a beautiful girl standing near the door to the school. "And Mariam. She was the best friend of Zahra. And I …"

The angel touched his shoulder and said,

"Go on… tell me."

"I loved her, you know." Karim's face blushed.

"But…"

"And the boys?"

"Mansour, my best friend. And Ali, the one who always stood up for me. The most loyal friend I had. Mansour came from a well to do family, whereas Ali and I were from poor families. But we went everywhere together. We were all in the same class at school. And afterwards, we would go up into the mountains nearby and look for wild berries, or fish in the stream. We were …"

"Yes?"

"… inseparable."

"And now?"

"Mansour is dead. Ali and Mariam, I gave them both jobs working in the factory…"

"Why do you longer speak to Ali and Mariam? asked the angel.

Karim looked down again. He shook his head. And said nothing.

"Come," said the angel. "We have to go."

Karim found himself once more high in the night sky. The moon shone down on them.

"Now," said the angel. "I regret that we must see something more painful."

This time they dropped down towards the house of Karim's childhood.

Karim recognised it instantly.

But this time the people inside it were not the same as before. There was a small crowd mostly wearing black.

In the parlour there were two coffins. Bodies covered with white sheets. All around were the mourners. The women were crying. The men were holding their tasbihs and praying. People were reciting Quran. Off in the corner were a teenage Karim, and Zahra.

"You remember this?" said the angel.

"The death of my parents," said Karim, choking.

"Cholera, wasn't it?" said the angel.

Karim nodded.

"And so, you became orphans, didn't you?"

"Yes."

Karim knew what was coming next.

"And yet you didn't want to give alms to Hajj Fawzi…"

"How did you know?"

"Surely Allah sees what you do."

"But I have given so much in the past. After I had finished investing in the new machines and making more profit, I had planned on giving some to him in the near future, I swear. I just hate getting bothered all the time with people asking for money, I'm not a bank you know…"

The angel replied simply:

"And never say of anything, 'Indeed I will do that tomorrow.'" (Quran 18:23).

Karim looked on with pain in his heart, thinking about his beloved parents.

"You and your twin sister went to live with your uncle Salim. So, you were taken care of. But it caused you to doubt, didn't it?"

"I could not understand why my parents, who were so kind and gentle, should be allowed to die, and leave us alone. It was not just. I prayed. But it …

"It hardened your heart?"

"Yes, Angel, it did. Of course, it did. The same would happen to anyone in my situation. I have seen enough," he said, turning away. "Take me back."

"Karim - you see things that give you great pain," said the angel, as they rose once more into the air.

"But don't despair. God is always with you."

This time as they descended it was into the town square. The sun was bright. They were outside a café.

There were five young people sitting there, under the big outdoor umbrellas, drinking coffee and eating sweet pastries.

"Whom do you see?" said the angel.

"Why, it is myself, as a young man." He pointed at the tall boy in the white suit. "I had been away to college in the capital by then."

"Tell me about it." said the Angel

"I was studying business with Mansour. You see him beside me." He pointed to the handsome man next to the younger Karim. "We were by then talking about setting up in business. Look, we are sharing figures about the factory."

"And the others?"

"Ali had become an accountant by that stage. He was always clever – good with numbers. And the girls – Mariam and Zahra," he pointed to the beautiful girl beside the young Karim, and to his sister, in a long sky-blue abaya, "They had become nurses. By then I had become engaged to Mariam. She was always my sweetheart. We planned to get married when I had enough money."

"And your destiny?"

"Why, Angel, I knew that it was to be a businessman. Mansour had money and I knew that he wanted to go into business. And I had the idea of a shoe factory."

"Why a shoe factory?" asked the angel.

"Because everyone needs shoes. If you can produce them at a good price, and sell them at a good margin, you will make money. Lots of money…"

"And making money was your destiny?"

Karim stopped and thought about it. Yes, indeed, after the death of his parents he had lost faith. If such things could happen in a cruel world, what could he rely on? He would make money. He would become a wealthy man.

"Why not?" said Karim, defensively.

"Is that the way of God?" said the angel.

"I personally think I have done very well with what money I have earned. God does not forbid us to make money …"

"No. But is it the most important thing in life?" asked the angel.

Karim walked up and down in the square, looking at his younger self.

"Perhaps not…. but it sure helps. I did what so many people do. I used my skills. And I improved the village. Half the village works in my factory. Without me they wouldn't even have a job."

"And did you want to give away any of the money you made?"

Karim said nothing. Then he snapped,

"Why do you judge me?"

"I do not judge you," said the angel. "Only God judges. I am just showing you."

Karim instantly regretted his outburst.

"Angel. I have seen enough. Please, take me back. I beg you."

"Karim - you see what you were, and you know what you have become. But don't despair. God is always with you."

They rose up into the air.

This time they alighted in front of the factory.

The sign was brand new. In gold letters, it proudly said, "Mansour and Malik."

"You were proud, weren't you?" said the angel.

"Yes. We had put everything into it. Mansour had his parents to help, but I had nothing but my brains and ideas. I'm sorry, am I boasting?"

The angel simply smiled.

They walked through the wall and into the main area of the factory. It was full of people, all hard at work. They were all happy.

Karim saw his old friend, Ali, sitting at a high desk, working on his figures. Tarek – another of his childhood friends - was the foreman. And there he was, with Mansour, watching over the workers.

Someone knocked at the door.

Mansour opened it. It was Hajj Fawzi. He was a little old man whose baldness told of his age and life experiences. He wore a white hat on his head and came to collect donations for the poor.

Karim saw his younger self frown. But Mansour whispered in his ear.

Mansour went up to the old man. Karim, looking on, trembled at what he was about to see.

But then the young Karim took out a little bag of money and upended it into Hajj Fawzi's open hand.

"So, you *did* know about charity," said the angel.

"Once, I did."

Hajj Fawzi bowed low and left the factory.

At that point, Mansour called out to the workers.

"It is the end of the Month of Ramadan," said he. "You have all worked hard this year. Let us stop now. You can all take the rest of the day off. Tomorrow is the great day of Eid. Prepare to meet up with your friends and family. And celebrate the greatness of God."

The workers all left the factory, laughing and singing. It was a time of joy and happiness.

The angel looked at Karim and said nothing.

They lifted up into the air.

Almost immediately, they dropped down in the nearby town square. It was still quite lovely. The war had not yet come to destroy it. On one side was the shining mosque, full of worshippers.

Opposite was an outdoor terrace. Two people were sitting at a table, sipping tea.

It was Mariam. And beside her was the young Karim.

"Your fiancée?"

"Yes."

"Then let us listen."

"Do we have to?"

The beautiful young woman was sitting beside Karim's younger self. But she had tears in her eyes.

"What has happened?" she asked him. "You said we would be married. I have now waited these five years. What have I done wrong?"

"Nothing," said the young Karim. "It's just that ..."

"Karim, we have known one another since childhood. When we were both poor. I accepted that you wanted to do something special. You and Mansour wanted to build up the business. I said I would wait. But ..."

"You must be patient."

"Karim," she said, taking his hand, "you have changed. Once all you said was how much you loved me, and how you wanted me to be your wife. But in recent times, you have scarcely looked at me. It seems that all you care about is money. Karim, when will you have enough?"

"Soon," he said.

"Karim. I must speak plainly. Once my love was all you wanted. And you had it. But these last years, all you seem to want is riches. Not love – gold. I no longer know you. You have changed from that sweet boy you were. You are on your way to becoming a greedy and cold man."

"Mariam. Please."

"I release you from your obligations," she said, standing up. "I do not wish to marry a man who cannot love. Consider yourself free. And may God have mercy on you."

She wiped away a tear, patted him on the shoulder, and left the square.

"Why did you do that?" said the angel. "You could have chosen the way of Hajj Fawzi. Or the way of Mansour, who understood charity. Or the way of Mariam, whom you once loved. Karim, you have made some bad choices."

"Bad choices," said Karim defensively. "All I did was to make our lives better. But she just couldn't see that. She just needed to wait a few more years and we would have been so comfortable that she would never have needed to work again. Angel… I feel that you are judging me again. Take me back home. I have seen enough. I cannot stand this anymore."

"Soon," said the angel, rising into the air again. "Don't despair Karim, Remember, God is always with you."

This time, they flew up high. The village was far below them. Karim looked down on its beautiful winding streets, the Kawthar River that ran through it, the white mosque, the charming houses, and in the valley beyond, the olive groves and small crops.

They set down on a mountaintop nearby.

"It was beautiful, was it not?" said the angel.

Down below, the village was picture perfect. The air was still. The sun shone warmly.

"Before the war, there was nowhere prettier," said Karim. "We all lived in peace, both communities, all of us together, and life was good."

"What happened?"

"I only know what I have been told. But it seems fighters came in from the war that was by then raging in the city. Both sides had militias. There were soldiers everywhere."

The sun went behind a cloud. The sound of engines rose in the still air. Convoys of trucks appeared in the streets. There was the sound of gunfire. Then an explosion. One of the houses was blown to bits. Fire and smoke rose into the air.

"Terrible things happened. There were killings. Not just men shooting at those on the other side but killing of women and children. Senseless killings."

"Why could you not all live in peace, as God has commanded?"

"Angel, I was not involved. After Mansour died, I stayed to look after the factory. Though I confess I felt anger at what the other side were doing. I too wanted to kill."

"Is that what God would want?"

"No. No. But… some of my workers gave up their jobs and went to fight. And I could understand why. There were stories of the greatest cruelty. Revenge. Murder. Atrocities. Ali was one of those who went to fight with his brothers in order to protect the village. During a battle Ali was hit in the knee by a bullet. Now he walks with a permanent limp… We've never spoken of what happened in the war although I must confess that I have heard many stories of his heroics and leadership during it. Even in the factory sometimes I hear the workers address him as the "General".

"Ali seems like an amazing man. Do you even speak to Ali anymore?"

Karim looked down without a word.

Below in the village, the scene of destruction went on. People running for their lives. Bodies in the streets. Buildings blown up. Smoke and dust everywhere. In a brief moment of silence, there rose the sound of screaming.

"This is not what God wants."

Karim hung his head and said nothing.

"Tell me about Zahra."

"I do not want to. Please. Not that. I have spoken about everything you have asked of me during this journey, but this is something I do not want to revisit... Please, Angel."

"You must, Karim."

The Angel had a presence and force that almost compelled Karim to speak against his will. He stood and looked into the distance. His face twisted with pain, and began…

"Zahra and Mariam had decided that they should help. As nurses they could lend assistance – help the wounded soldiers and civilians - put together a field hospital. Do good."

"And…?" asked the angel.

"But how could I risk losing my only sister? How could I take that chance? She was all I had left after my parents' death. I loved her more than life itself."

"You tried to keep her safe?"

"Yes. Yes of course. I tried to. I would die for her."

And as he said those words, he was taken back in time to one of their last conversations together. They were sitting at the same kitchen table – the one of their first Ramadan. Sitting across from one another. He reached out and took her hand.

"Please don't go," I begged her. "Stay home. At least here, you'll be away from the worst of the conflict. If Mariam wants to go, let her."

"Karim, I must do this," she replied. "There is so much death and injury. I will be doing a good thing. I will be helping those in need of aid. It is my duty to the people of Al Tawbah and to God."

"I tried to make her see reason. To no avail. Then I tried to threaten her.

"If you do this," I yelled, "I will no longer be your brother! I swear it. I will cast you aside!"

"At this, she leapt up from the table, crying. She ran from the room.

"I went after her, catching her before she could leave the house. I had never said or done anything that would hurt my beloved sister. She was the apple of my eyes, my pride and joy.

"No. No. I don't mean it."

"I held her in an embrace.

"Zahra, I love you so much. I can't have you dying too. Not after what we have already been through."

"I gently placed a kiss on her forehead.

"Stay with me. I will protect you"

Karim found that his own eyes were wet with the memory of it.

"She went?" asked the angel.

"Yes. I begged her to stay with me, but she didn't listen. For months she was safe. She and Mariam were together, normally far from the fighting. The war sometimes came up into our valley, but often it was far off. They established a field hospital in the school – it was still standing, unlike most of the other buildings in Al Tawbah. There were plenty of rooms, and all classes had been cancelled because of the fighting.

"The last day I saw her, she came to the factory. She was wearing her sky-blue hijab. She always wore it as it reminded her of our parents' love. She brought me a simple meal of baba ghanoush, with pita bread. We sat in the board room and laughed about old times. She was full of praise for Mariam, who was working so hard to help the wounded. She said, 'This war must surely finish soon. We are fighting people we know. Often old friends. It is madness.'"

"I was so pleased to see her that I agreed, though in my heart I felt that she was being too optimistic about how long it would last. When people are capable of so much hate, it is hard to put a stop to it. We had by then both lost friends in the conflict. There had been so much blood.

"She kissed me goodbye and said she was going back to the hospital. I walked with her to the door and I waved to her as she went down the street. She smiled and waved back.

"In the distance, I heard a loud bang. I said to my foreman, 'What is it?' He replied, 'Some of the fighters have come into the town again. They are looking for our militia.'

"I went back to work. Why did I not go after her? She was only a few streets away. I had said I would protect her. Instead, I went back to my figures, my calculations, my obsession with money. For some reason it never occurred to me that Zahra could be hurt. Why would anyone hurt a nurse who is helping those in need?

"Only half an hour later, a girl came rushing into the factory. 'Where is Mr Malik?' she was screaming, between sobs, 'It is his sister…'

"I knew then that something was wrong. I ran as fast as I could to the hospital.

"In the emergency room were a doctor and several nurses. And on the table, Zahra. She was covered in blood.

"'What happened?" I cried.

"'A stray bullet from the other militia. She had been called out and was helping a stretcher crew carry the wounded back. No one knows who. But she was walking and talking one moment, and the next lying in the dust.'

"I went closer to her. Behind her was Mariam. We looked at each other. Mariam was vainly trying to stem the flow of blood. I looked into Mariam's eyes, and I saw only terror and fear. There was nothing they could do to save her.

"Zahra," I cried out, kneeling beside her. "Please … please … please don't go. Zahra!"

"She looked at me. She was wearing the sky-blue abaya that our mother had gifted her years ago. It was covered in blood. She looked at me with a look of love so profound that my heart ached. She smiled. She touched my head. I kissed her hand.

"And then … she … she died."

"The very next day, we walked behind her coffin. All the village was there. We walked from one side of Al Tawbah to the other, all the way to the cemetery, to bury her next to my father and mother."

Karim sat down on the mountain, his head in his hands. He wept without cease.

"No, Karim," said the angel, "*here* you acted as you should. With love."

"How?" said Karim, wiping away his tears.

"You tried to protect her. You went to her as she died. You showed her that you loved her. And she you. And you buried her in the proper way. She is dead, it's true. But we must all die one day."

"But she should not have died! It is not fair! She is gone now, gone forever. She has left me all alone."

And Karim wept again.

"It has made you cold, hasn't it?"

"YES. Why should I not be cold, when those I love are taken from me? What is the point of life? There is too much suffering. Too many deaths. She was the most perfect person I had ever known, and now she too was gone. I felt I could not go on."

"But you did, didn't you? You turned away from people to…"

"Money. Yes. And why not? I couldn't feel any more. I did not want to suffer any more."

"But in shutting out pain, you also shut out life and those you loved and cared for."

Karim looked at the angel.

"SHE IS GONE, OKAY!" he snarled. "NOTHING YOU DO OR SAY WILL CHANGE THAT!"

"She died in the way of God," said the angel. "She is a martyr, always remember:

"And reckon not those who are killed in Allah's way as dead: nay, they are alive (and) are provided sustenance from their Lord" (Quran 3:169)

"Know that your sister is always with you. You just have to have faith and see the signs. They are everywhere if you open your eyes. And open your heart.

The angel beckoned.

"Come, Karim. Our journey is over. I am taking you back home, as you requested."

Within seconds, Karim was back in his bed chamber.

He climbed into bed, wiping his eyes, in a daze between reality and illusion.

"Karim, you made some bad choices, it's true," said the angel. "But it was not *all* bad. You loved your parents. You loved your sister. You *did* have a good heart."

"What next?"

"I am going whence I came. But shortly you will have another visitor. Pay heed to him. Go with him as he shows you things. And most important, learn from him."

"Angel," said Karim, "stay with me."

"My time is up," said the angel. "But these are my final words, and they are important: No matter how bad things seem, God is always with you."

With that, the angel swept out of the room.

His brilliant light got smaller and smaller as he ascended off into the night sky. Soon all Karim could see was a tiny dot of light, in the beautifully still night sky.

At that, exhausted, Karim laid back and fell asleep.

The Second Angel

he clock struck two.

Karim woke.

He sat up and looked around.

He was alone in his bed chamber.

What's the matter with me? he thought.

First, I imagine that Mansour has come back from the dead.

Then I dream that an angel comes to visit me. And he takes me on a journey into the past.

He climbed out of bed. Walked up and down nervously.

His conversations with the angel were coming back to him now. He had been transported …

Back to himself as a child – the time of his first Month of Ramadan – and his mother and father and his sister Zahra.

Back to his days at school, and his childhood friends.

Back to – he shuddered as he recalled it – the death of his parents.

And to his scheme, with his good friend Mansour, to open a shoe factory.

And then … Mariam … He had loved Mariam, but she had left him.

Why?

"You are on your way to becoming a greedy and cold man."

Was it true?

It was. He had become bitter, he knew.

He stopped pacing and thought about the war.

The decision by Mariam and Zahra to help out as nurses.

His bitter words to Zahra.

And then …

The death of his beloved sister.

"It has made you cold," the angel had said.

Yes. It had. He had lost his business partner, his parents, and his twin sister. Why should he care anymore, about anyone?

He went to the window. The crescent moon was hanging high in the sky.

Karim stared at it. Was it a dream? Had he really talked to an angel? Why did he feel somehow different?

He looked at the golden moon.

Then he saw something.

It's happening again, he thought. He stood back, half in terror, half in excitement.

Near to the moon was a second star. He looked at it. It was getting bigger.

He clutched his gown around him and retreated inside the room.

Sure enough, the light was getting brighter and brighter.

A shining light was before him. It glowed brighter and brighter.

Karim knelt down and raised his hands in prayer.

"Karim," said the angel, "I am here on a heavenly mission. I was sent to help you."

"Who are you?" said Karim, daring to raise his eyes.

"I am the Angel of the Ramadan of the Present," said the angel. "I have come to show you things you need to see."

"But Angel. Why me? … I understand that I am not perfect and have made mistakes, but who hasn't? I am a good man. I don't deserve this. I want to be left alone…"

"Are you a good man?" said the angel. "We will see. Come!"

And he held out his hand.

Together they moved out the window, and up into the night sky.

Once more, Karim found himself high above the village of Al Tawbah.

It was the time of the breaking of the fast. It was the previous evening. Karim recognised the scene immediately.

They gently descended toward the village hall. Then they were inside.

The hall was full of Karim's workers and their families – their wives and children. The women had been busy. Despite the shortages, there was a wonderful feast for the last iftar of the month of Ramadan. The tables were covered with food: kibbeh, kafta, manakish, lentil soup, fatoush and tabouleh. There were urns of hot water for tea. There were plates of sweet maamoul and shaabiyat and baklava.

Karim and the Angel stood by the wall.

No one could see them, but they could see and hear everything.

"Who was that who came in the door just now and then went off?" said one of the women.

Karim pricked up his ears. He moved closer and found to his dismay that he was standing next to Mariam.

She was still as beautiful as ever. But her face had a terribly sad look to it.

"Oh, that was Karim Malik."

"Mr. Malik! The boss from hell! That awful man!"

They all laughed.

"He's a monster," said one of the other women. "We all hate him, don't we?" And she looked around at her companions, who nodded agreement.

"He's so mean," said another. "I can't believe it. He works us so hard. He pays us as little as he can. He never gives to the poor. He's a shocking miser."

"Worse still," said another, "He thinks himself so high and mighty. As if because he's made a lot of money, it makes him a good man. It doesn't."

They all laughed.

"He's getting his reward already. His wealth is no use to him. He can't do any good with it. He's a miserable man – you can see it in his face."

"You know he lives all alone," said another. "In that grand house just up the hill. He bought it on the cheap from one of the old families. They'd gone broke. He could have given them a good price. But he's too greedy. It's no secret - he took advantage of them."

"I know. No one would want to marry him.

Surely …"

There was a sudden silence.

They all looked at Mariam.

"Didn't you …?"

Mariam looked down at her food.

She took a sip of tea, and said, gently,

"He used to be such a good person; besides we should not be backbiting, it is a grave sin, especially on such a holy night."

"But are we not saying the truth?"

"If it were not true then it would be a graver sin", replied Mariam solemnly.

"Weren't you once … engaged?"

Mariam nodded.

"You don't mean he abandoned you?"

"No. No. I let him go."

"What? A man that rich? Why?"

"Because … because he was no longer the man I fell in love with. I knew by then it wouldn't work."

"But you could have been rich too. And the mistress of that great house."

"Why get married if there is no love?"

No one had anything to say to that.

"But I hope," said Mariam, "that one day he will change. And become again the man I loved."

Karim shrunk back against the wall. He put his hands over his head.

Then he turned to the angel and said,

"Angel, she could have waited a few more years…. We were going to be married. And foolishly she threw it all away. She said to me once, 'It seems all that you care about is money.'"

"Is she right?"

"No. *Yes.* I guess so. But why not? What else can you rely on? People talk about goodness and kindness. But those things don't put food on the table. Being nice doesn't give people jobs."

The angel said nothing. He just pointed, indicating to Karim to turn his head. A man was coming towards Mariam.

"Who is that?"

"Ali. The oldest of my friends."

"Then let us listen."

Ali limped towards Mariam and the other women and placed his walking stick on the floor. He carefully sat down.

"We were talking about Mr. Malik," said the woman who had called Karim a monster. "You've known him a long time, haven't you?"

"We were all childhood friends," said Ali. "Karim, Mansour, and me. As well as Mariam and… Zahra."

"Has he always been this horrible?"

"He has suffered a lot," said Ali. "His parents both died. Then Zahra was killed in the war and now he has a factory to run on his own, without Mansour. He has a lot of responsibility. Don't be too hard on him."

"You're too forgiving," said one. "You always defend Malik".

"And what are we commanded?" said Ali. "*Surely, God forgives all sins. Indeed, He is the most forgiving, the merciful…*"

"Does Malik even *believe* in God?" asked one of the women. "He doesn't even fast anymore. I saw him drinking tea today."

"As a boy, he was as devout as his father and mother. He went to mosque every day. He was as kind a boy I ever have known."

"And now?" asked the woman.

Ali was silent. He looked down at his hands, then at Mariam.

"*Do* you believe in God?" said the angel to Karim.

Karim turned away and hid his face against the wall. He felt his eyes welling up with tears.

He had travelled so far from his childhood now. He had made all the money in the world. But had he lost his soul?

The angel tapped him on the shoulder. Ali was speaking again.

"Karim Malik is my oldest friend," said Ali. "He has gone through the sort of trials most of us never know. You think of him as cold and unfeeling. But I know otherwise. Inside Karim there is still that kind boy, who loved his parents and his sister…" he looked at Mariam, "and Mariam."

"Perhaps it's not too late," said Mariam. "After all, it's the last night of the month of Ramadan. Tomorrow is Eid. This is a time when miracles happen."

"Then let us all say a du'a for him," said Ali. "Let us ask God for help. Let us pray that his heart will soften, and he that will find his faith again.

"Call on me, I will answer you" (Quran 40:60)

And with that, they all bowed their heads in prayer.

The angel took Karim by the hand and led him away.

"That," said the angel, "is real love."

"Angel, you've got me wrong! I swear I was going to give them all a small pay rise once we bought the new machines. I have a business to run. Life is tough. I have the whole weight of the world on my shoulders… Why am I here? What do you want me to do?"

"Karim – you know what you must do."

"What? Should I speak to them?"

"Not now. There's still more to see."

Karim felt himself lifted up into the air. They rose above the village once again.

Far below, they could see a child in the street.

A tall man in a dark suit went by, weaving in and out of the piles of rubble from the broken buildings.

"Please," said the child to the man, holding up a hand, "could you spare a penny?"

But the man put his head down and kept going, pretending he didn't see the child.

"Who is that man?" said the angel.

The piteous cry of the child reached Karim and the Angel.

Karim realised that it was himself.

The man went on down the street.

Suddenly, there was the call to prayer. The sound from the minaret echoed across the village and into the valley beyond.

"Oh no, not that," said the man as he looked up at the mosque. He hurried on.

"Who is that man?" said the angel.

Karim knew that it was himself.

Shortly after, the Angel and Karim alighted by a small building in a poorer part of town.

Many of the buildings had been shattered by bombs during the war. But this one had been spared. In the old days, before the fighting, it had been a small shop. Karim could not remember what it sold. But the owner was long gone – possibly killed.

They stood, Karim and the angel, looking in through the glass of the shop front. A cloth covered the windows as a shield, to cover what was happening inside. But through a gap beside the fabric Karim and the angel could see a single lamp glowing at the back.

At that moment, a young woman came down the street and stopped at the shop.

It was Mariam. She went in.

"Oh no," said Karim. "Please."

"Was she not dear to you?" said the angel.

"Yes. Perhaps I should have been more patient with her – showed her the error of her ways."

"She is on her own," said the angel. "Why?"

"Because she never married… after… I… after she and I stopped seeing one another."

"And yet she is here with a purpose. Shall we see what it is?"

They followed Mariam inside.

It was a scene of activity. The small space was filled with people – desperate people.

One woman was having her child examined. He was obviously very ill. Karim was reminded of the child in the street – the one begging for pennies. This child was clearly in need of food. Karim realised that this was the same child that he had walked by. The boy was shivering violently - chilled from the cold winter's night.

Mariam came in and spoke.

"How are we going?"

Karim recognised the nurses. He had gone to high school with most of them and he knew them well. They had all joined the field hospital that Mariam and his sister had put together during the war. Here they were once again working hard for the greater cause…. And was there any better cause? he thought to himself.

One of the nurses pointed to the shelf with its jars of medicines and remedies.

"We're almost out of so many things. We desperately need more money to buy supplies. We're even short of bandages."

"What is this place?" said Karim to the angel.

"It is a small medical clinic that she set up after the war. These women all have other jobs. The nurses help people after hours, for that's all they can afford. But they are desperate for money. They need help."

"Then why don't they ask for it?"

At this point, one of the young women said to Mariam,

"I went to the factory and asked to see Mr. Malik. But his supervisor, Rami, when he heard what I wanted, said, 'This is a business, young woman. Can't you see I'm busy? Mr. Malik supports all his workers – as long as they work hard. He's not a charity! He doesn't want to pay for other people's children as well.'"

"Did you see Mr. Malik?"

"No. Rami sent me away."

Mariam opened her bag and pulled out some money.

"Here," she said to her assistant Fatima. Take this and buy what you need."

"But we need morphine," said the other woman. "It's very expensive."

"For whom?"

"For the little boy with the terrible pain."

"For Zain?"

"Yes. But this is most of your wage. How will you live?"

"I'll be fine. I can't stand by and let him suffer like that."

At this point, the angel took Karim by the hand and made to go.

"Wait," said Karim. "Zain. I know that name. I must find out…"

"You will," said the angel. "Come with me."

As they got up to leave, they saw a large sign hanging on the wall. It simply said; "Zahra Malik Medical Clinic". Underneath was a large picture of Karim's beautiful sister and a verse from the Holy Quran which read,

"And reckon not those who are killed in Allah's way as dead: nay they are alive (and are provided sustenance from their Lord)." (Quran 3:169)

Karim realised that this was the same verse from the Holy Quran that the previous angel had quoted. Karim could hold back no more. Tears filled his eyes.

"My beautiful sister… I miss her so much…"

"She has never left you, Karim. She is alive with everyone. The signs are everywhere. Could it be any clearer?"

"What have I become?" he said to the angel. "They are here working for free and saving people's lives and I am…" He couldn't go on.

"It's never too late to change," said the angel. "See this as a reminder of what love looks like. Do you want to be a good man?"

"Yes! Yes!"

"Then learn. And change."

This time, they didn't go very far.

The angel stopped only a few houses away, an even shabbier building than the one they had just seen.

Karim wondered if he knew the house. Much of Al Tawbah had been destroyed and he wasn't sure anymore. Then he realised with a start whose house it was.

"Please, Angel," he said. "I don't want to go in there. I have a really bad feeling."

"Karim, you need to."

And suddenly they were inside Ali's house.

It was a poor place, with small, crowded rooms. The walls were bare.

The angel led him into a small bedroom. There were two beds.

On one sat a little girl. On the other lying down, was a little boy. He was deathly pale, and in obvious pain. The mother and father were sitting beside him, while his sister looked on. She was quietly weeping.

The mother was trying to feed him some soup. But he didn't want any. His eyes were open wide with pain.

"Who are these people, Karim?" asked the angel.

"It is Ali," said Karim. "My old friend. And his wife, Hanna, the sister of Mariam. The little girl is his daughter Jana."

"And what is wrong with the boy?" asked the angel.

"I don't know," moaned Karim. "Since the war, I have not had anything to do with them. But whatever it is - it looks bad."

At this point someone else came into the room.

It was Mariam.

They all said Salaam, and Hanna kissed Mariam on the cheek.

She sat by the boy. She held up a small vile and a syringe.

"It is the last of what we have," she said. "But I have ordered more. I gave instructions tonight for new supplies, and other medicines we need."

"Will it cure the disease?" said Ali.

"No. But it will help with the pain," replied Mariam. "I'm afraid that's all I can do without the help of a surgeon."

"But we can't afford one," said Ali.

Mariam gently pushed a needle into the vile. In the feeble light of the lamp, Karim saw her draw the liquid into the syringe. Then, with practiced hands, she administered the injection.

"God bless us, everyone," said the boy.

Zain laid back in his bed.

Everyone was watching him nervously.

The boy's eyes closed.

He finally fell asleep.

At that point, Hanna embraced her sister Mariam. And their tears flowed freely.

Karim found that his own eyes were overflowing too.

"But what can I do?" he sobbed. "I was there when he was born. It was in the old days, and I was still talking to Ali."

"Your friend, you said? Then why did you treat him like this?"

Karim heard his own voice in his head:

"I tell you what," he said, *"you can take the Sunday off."*

"But sir, that's our normal day of rest."

"Exactly. You can wait. Off you go. And don't interrupt again, if you want to keep your job!"

"Was that you?" said the Angel.

"Yes. Yes. Oh, Angel. What have I become? Why did Mariam not come to *me* to ask for money? She named the clinic after my sister and never even told me!"

"Karim, you know why she didn't come. Be honest."

Karim heard the voice of Rami again:

"Now that it is Eid, do you think we should donate a little to Hajj Fawzi, the kind man who helps the poor? There are so many orphans, and he is feeding them. We are making a lot of money. What do you think?"

And his reply:

"Don't be stupid! I've given enough to him over the years. And I pay enough taxes to this corrupt government. Why should I care? We don't need religion. We don't need to give away anything. We need to build the business and save up for more machines so we can produce even more shoes."

"Was that you, Karim?"

"Yes, it was. I have sinned, haven't I? How can I make amends? Could God forgive me?"

At this, the angel looked Karim in the eyes. A heavenly light shone. Karim looked down. The angel said,

"Even if your sins are countless, God's mercy is endless. God forgives all sins."

"Even me?" said Karim.

"Even you."

Within seconds, Karim was back in his bed chamber.

He climbed into bed. His heart was still sore with what he had seen.

"Karim, you now know what people think of you. Can you blame them?"

Karim looked down and said nothing.

"And you have seen what Mariam has done. She, unlike you, shows faith and love."

Karim nodded.

"I loved her," he whispered.

"Good. Then hear again what she said:

"But I have every hope that he will one day change. And become again the man I loved."

"We are blessed by God in so many ways," said the angel. "Always remember that and be grateful."

Karim nodded and held up his palms in an attitude of prayer.

"You have learnt something, I see," said the angel. "I am going now. Soon you will have another visitor. Pay heed to him. He will show you things you need to know… if you *are* to become a good man again."

"Angel," said Karim, "stay with me. I need advice. I want to make good, but I don't know how."

"Alas. My time is up," said the angel. "Listen to these words: *Do not despair of the mercy of Allah. Indeed, Allah forgives all sins. (39.35)*

No matter how bad things seem; God is always with you."

With that, the angel swept out of the room.

His brilliant light got smaller and smaller in the night sky.

Soon all Karim could see was a second brightly shining star far in the distance.

The Third Angel

The clock struck three.

Karim woke again.

He sat up and thought about what had happened.

Another foolish dream. Another angel. And more absurd accusations against his good name. The words came back to him:

"He's a monster… We all hate him, don't we?"

"He's a miserable man. You can see it in his face."

"No one would want to marry him…"

And Mariam:

"Why get married if there is no love?"

That hurt. She *had* thrown away a chance to have it all. What did she want? He was rich enough.

At least Ali had defended him.

"Inside Karim is still that kind boy… Let us pray that his heart will soften, and that he will find his faith again."

Karim walked to the window and peered at the night sky. The two brightly shining stars were almost conversing with him.

Had he lost his faith? Had he become cold and cruel?

"It's never too late to change… Do you want to be a good man?"

Yes, he did. Of course, he did. He was making excuses – protesting his goodness when he knew deep down what a cold, heartless man he had become.

Then he thought about the other things he had seen:

The cold boy begging in the street.

The same child shivering in the clinic with his mother.

And then – worst of all:

The humble house of his old friend Ali. Hanna, Jana, and the sick boy, Zain, his friend's only son.

Mariam giving the child an injection of pain relief to stop the pain. And the child's words:

"God bless us, everyone."

By now, Karim was shivering. It was not the cold. It was fear.

He had been living his life trying to keep away more deaths. Trying to protect himself against pain. Putting off life, turning away from love. And religion. And getting more miserable day by day.

He remembered a saying by one of the members of the Holy Prophet's family that he had loved as a boy: "O Lord, what did he find who lost you and what did he lose who found you?" He thought to himself, "I have found nothing since turning away from God."

"KARIM!" said a loud voice.

He almost fell to the floor.

He turned.

A huge figure was standing behind him. It was hooded. It was wearing a long black robe. It glowed with a terrible red light. Karim looked up into the face of the angel.

But there was no face. Just an empty space.

"Oh please," whispered Karim, falling to his knees, "please spare me. You are the Angel of Death, aren't you?"

"No," said the figure, "I am the Angel of the Ramadan of the Future."

"What future?"

"Your future, Karim. Come!"

And they flew out into the night sky.

Clouds had now blanketed the night sky completely. It was very dark outside.

They descended into a wide-open space. Fog swirled everywhere. All around were strange ghostly shapes, like white pillars standing out of the ground.

"Where are we?" said Karim.

"A place of death," said the angel. He pointed his long bony figure at Karim. "Once death arrives, you will beg to return. But by then it's too late."

"Beg to return?"

"To have your life over again. To make amends. To love. To become a good man."

"But I…" began Karim. Then he thought about what he had seen that night. He had avoided the beggar boy. He had refused alms to Hajj Fawzi. He had treated his oldest friend with contempt. He had not even known that Ali's son was so sick. He had allowed Mariam, whom he had loved, to be alone when he could have…"

The clouds parted, and suddenly, in the light of the stars, Karim could see where they were.

There were in the graveyard of Al Tawbah. All around them were silent white tombstones. The fog swirled around the gravestones. Overhead, the clouds rushed by.

Karim stumbled back against a newly dug grave. He scrambled to his feet, panting.

"Why are we here? I'm not dead, am I?"

"Not yet."

"What do you mean?"

"Karim, like all men you have too short a life. What you do with the years that God has given you is what counts."

"Take me back," cried Karim, clutching at the angel. "I know now I have done wrong. I want to do better. Please."

"How serious are you?" asked the angel.

"I promise," said Karim. "I want to change."

"We will see," said the angel.

At that point, Karim heard a noise. He had thought they were alone in the cemetery. But not far off were voices.

He looked. Not far away, he saw a man, two women and a young girl. They were standing at a tombstone, praying.

"Who are they?"

"I think you know."

"Angel, take me back. I have seen enough. I don't want to know."

"You must go to them," said the angel. And he led Karim towards them.

To his shock, Karim realised who they were.

Ali was standing with his wife Hanna by the side of the grave. It was a new headstone. Beside Hanna was the girl, Jana. The girl stooped to put a football on the grave.

"It's his birthday," she said. "A present for him."

Her mother burst into tears. Ali placed his arms around her in attempt to give her some comfort.

Then the other woman came forward. It was Mariam. She knelt by the grave and put flowers on it. She took out her Quran and began to recite some of its verses.

"Whose grave is it?" asked Karim.

"I think you know," said the angel.

Karim moved closer. The fog lifted briefly.

On the tombstone, just below the crescent, was the name:

"Zain Akeel."

"He died?" said Karim, choking.

"Of course. We all die."

"But he was so young. *Too* young."

"He was in pain. Did you help the boy? His father was your friend. Did you help him? Your former love tended to him. Did you give her aid?"

"No! No! No!"

Karim covered his head with his hands.

"Could I have helped?"

"You know full well you could have."

"How?"

"You are a rich man, Karim. You could have given his parents the money to go to the big city and get the best possible care. You could have shown your love for your old friend in a way that might have made a difference."

"But I did not know he was ill. I swear."

"And *why* did you not know?"

Karim stood up and looked across at the grieving family. He wiped a tear from his eye.

"They did not tell me!"

"Why not?"

"Because…"

But then he remembered his words about Hajj Fawzi. And his comments to Ali. And his abandonment – for that's what it was – of Mariam.

"No one told you, "Said the angel, "because everyone knew that your heart was cold."

"But," said Karim, weeping now, "I did not know the child was going to die. I never wanted that. I would have helped if I had known…"

"Did you help the beggar boy?"

"No."

"Did you go to the mosque and pray to become a better man?"

"No."

"Then how can I believe your words about the dead child?"

"Please!" cried Karim, kneeling.

"I told you, did I not, that you would beg to return to fix things once death arrives? But by then it is too late."

"I wish to make amends," Karim pleaded. "Please."

He stood up and went towards the family by Zain's grave. He held out his hands to Ali.

But he was invisible.

Ali took the hands of Hanna and Jana, and slowly led them away.

"Please," called Karim, going after them. "You should have told me."

Mariam stood up from the grave and made to follow Ali and his family.

"Mariam," said Karim. "You should have told me. I could have helped. I owed that to Ali, and to you."

Mariam wiped her eyes and followed the others.

She looked back at the graveyard. It was empty of any living soul.

"Come," said the angel. "There is something more."

He led Karim away.

"Please. I don't want to see any more. I want to go home."

"But Karim… This is your home," said the angel.

"What on earth do you mean?"

"Behold," said the angel. And he pointed.

Two men had come silently into the cemetery. They were dressed all in black. They were carrying a wooden casket and making their way slowly towards a newly dug grave.

They arrived, and carefully lowered the coffin to the ground nearby.

As he approached, he could hear them talking.

"That was so heavy!" said one. "Thank God we have arrived."

They sat down beside the grave to rest.

"Why are we here on our own?" said the other. "Where are the mourners? Where is the family? Is the dead man from out of town?"

"I don't know. I heard that he was rich. But no one liked him. He never married. He lived alone. It was his housekeeper who found him dead in his bed. No send off. She got someone to give him his final cleansing and then wrapped his body. That's all I know."

"Well, we were paid to bring him. And to bury him. I don't care who he was. We will do our duty."

"Who *was* this man?" Karim asked the angel.

"Who do you think?"

"Angel, this could have been me. I was cold. I never married. I scorned religion."

The angel said nothing.

"But I am not dead. I am still young. Too young to die."

"How do you know? What about Mansour? What about your parents? What about Zahra?"

At this, Karim froze. It was not possible. Was it?

The two men stood up.

They reached into the casket, one at each end, and carefully lifted out the body.

In the faint light of the moon, Karim could see the shape of a man, shrouded in the white kafan, tied on each end.

They lowered it slowly into the grave. Karim looked down at the shape that had once been a man like himself.

"But who is it?"

The angel pointed at the new tombstone.

It was hard to make out in the darkness. Karim went closer. And closer.

The first letter was a K. The surname began with M.

Karim shrunk back in horror.

"Take me back," he begged. "I want to repent. I want to do right. Please."

"I told you that you would beg to return when death came, did I not? Now that death is here it is too late."

"But surely," pleaded Karim, "this must be the shape of things that might be, not of what must be? If I changed, surely this would not be the end?"

The angel remained silent.

At that moment, shapes emerged from the darkness, circling the grave. They were like giant beasts, which frightened Karim, but the cemetery workers were neither troubled nor afraid. Only Karim could see these terrifying beasts. He could see their white tusks, gleaming in the faint light as they closed in on the body.

"What are they?" cried Karim, terrified.

"They are your evil deeds coming to haunt you."

"Please. Please. What will protect me?"

"Good deeds. But will you have enough?"

"Angel, I don't want to die. I have too much to live for."

"Really?"

"My old friend. And his family. And all my workers. And Mariam…"

But it was too late.

All at once, he found himself at the bottom of the grave.

He was lying on his back, inside a white shroud. It was tied top and bottom. He could not move.

"NO! NO!"

The men standing by the graveside began to throw earth into the grave. They went about it slowly, shovel by shovel.

The light of the stars was hidden by the clouds. But Karim could see the pile of earth around him getting higher every second.

He felt the dirt mounting up around him. They were burying him.

"NO! PLEASE!" he cried out. "I have learnt my lesson. I know I have sinned. I know I have been cruel. I don't want to die!"

Now he could barely see. The dirt had now nearly filled up the newly dug grave. The weight of it on his body was awful. He could no longer move. The last of the light was almost gone. Karim was desperate. He called out wildly,

"PLEASE!"

Suddenly, he heard a voice. A voice he knew.

A figure came into sight. A woman. She was standing at the foot of the grave, looking down. She was weeping.

"MARIAM!" he cried out. 'It's me, Karim. Help me, please."

She wiped her tears.

She stooped and picked up a clod of earth.

She said a prayer for his soul.

Then she threw the earth in on top of him. This was to be the dirt that finally filled up Karim's grave. How ironic and sad that it would be thrown in by his one true love, that he had pushed away because of his despondent and forlorn ways.

At that moment all light was gone.

He could see nothing at all. The weight of the earth on him was unbearable.

Karim was all alone in his grave.

He could sense the beasts all around him. He could hear their awful noises as they prepared to rip into him. He could feel their foul breath upon him.

Scared, frightened, regretful, remorseful, and all alone, in the dark... Karim knew that it was only his good deeds that could save him now.

Had he done enough in his life?

The Miracle

K arim woke up.

It was pitch black.

"I am dead," he thought. "I have gone to hell. I deserved it, of course. I was heartless. No one loved me because I didn't love anyone else. I was a bad man."

He stopped.

He could make out strange shapes in the darkness.

It was not the grave.

It was his bedroom.

He turned sideways. There was his side table. And his window. Through the window the night sky. The night sky was once again highlighting its starts. Three in particular shone brightly.

I AM NOT DEAD!" he yelled. "I am alive. I AM ALIVE!"

He leapt out of bed. He clutched his arms around himself - and danced with joy.

"I am so happy!" he called out, clapping his hands, and skipping about the room like a child. "I have been given a second chance. Oh Merciful God, it's not too late. I will do better this time. I will change the man I had become; into a man you would want me to be."

He remembered the Angel's words:

"I told you that you would beg to return when death came..."

And his own:

"If I changed, surely this would not be the end."

"I am not dead! I have learnt my lesson. I will become that kind boy again. I promise. God be praised."

In a buzz of excitement, Karim went to his wardrobe, and took out his best clothes. He found himself singing with happiness.

He went into the bathroom and showered with an intention of purification. An intention of being born again. He put on his clothes, brushed his hair and in a state of absolute bliss, he rushed out of the door.

It was still slightly dark outside. A cold morning, shortly before dawn. The village was utterly silent.

Karim headed through the streets as fast as he could go.

He arrived at the house.

He stopped and composed his face.

He knocked on the door.

Nothing.

He knocked again.

From inside, he could hear someone stirring.

He knocked a third time.

Someone on the other side of the door called out, "Who is it?"

"IT'S YOUR BOSS. OPEN UP IMMEDIATELY!"

The door opened slowly. Ali's face, still half asleep, appeared in the half light.

"Why sir… Mr. Malik. What is it?"

"Ali. You must come to work early with me," said Karim.

"But sir. It's nearly prayer time. What are you doing here at this hour?"

"We have a special delivery coming in from the city," said Karim sharply. "You must come with me to the factory right now. Get dressed. I'll wait. And be quick."

Ali hurried back inside to do as he was ordered.

Still the same man, Ali thought to himself. He is getting worse as every year passes. Just as cold as ever. Just as demanding.

He dressed quickly, put on his warmest coat, for it was icy cold, and joined Karim on the street.

Minutes later, they were on their way to the main part of Al Tawbah. On one side of the street was the mosque. On the other side was the factory.

"Yesterday," said Karim, "you said you wanted me to close the factory for Eid. Do you realise how much we would lose if we did such a thing?"

Ali walked on with his head down and said nothing.

"I guess you think you could run the business," said Karim, "Am I right? So, tell me - if you were involved in running Malik Shoes, how would you make it better?"

They stopped. Ali looked carefully at his boss. In a quiet voice he said,

"Sir, you might not like what I have to say. I will keep silent."

"No. Go on. Say what you have to say. I'm listening."

"Our shoes are good. But they could be better. We could make sure that the stitching is finer, and the finish on the leather more shiny. And a bigger range. They are good shoes. They could be great."

"I see," said Karim, frowning. "How would these things be done then? What's the problem?"

"Your workers are not happy, sir. Forgive me for saying it, but they think you treat them as slaves."

"Nonsense," snorted Karim. "They are paid what they should be paid, no more and no less. This is not some sort of charity, Ali."

"Mr Malik. This is not just a business. It is not just about money. May I suggest that you pay them what they deserve. Treat them with… with respect… with love."

"How would that help?"

"In return they will work with joy in their hearts. They will work harder. They will produce more. And they will help you make better shoes. I know it. They are after all, your brothers and sisters under God. If they feel that love and respect, then I guarantee we will in fact improve our quality and double our sales. Now that's how you should run your factory," said Ali passionately.

And then he continued

"We must always remember what the holy Quran says about this:

"Allah may give them the best reward of what they have done and give them more out of His grace; and Allah gives sustenance to whom he pleases without measure." (Quran 24:38)

"Don't forget, it is He and only He who gives you what you have. You are lucky that you have so much wealth. Give of it, be kinder. I promise God will give you more in return…"

Karim was silent.

"Forgive me Sir," said Ali. "I have said too much."

Karim looked directly at Ali and said in a soft voice,

"Those are the last words you will ever say as my employee."

Ali went cold with fear.

They had arrived at the factory. Karim took a key from his coat and opened the door.

"Come with me!' he ordered.

He led the way to the board room. He lit the lamps.

"Sit! I have some news for you."

Ali felt his heart sinking. Was I not grateful enough? What had he done that Mr. Malik was going to fire him? His breath raced. Without a job, how could he feed his family? They would all starve. He would plead. He would beg.

He looked over at his childhood friend. Karim's face was completely blank. He was writing something on a piece of paper. How cruel can he be, given our shared history, thought Ali.

"Read it," commanded Karim. Passing him a paper.

Ali could barely see the words. The paper trembled in his hands.

And this is what he read:

To Ali Akeel,

Be it known that from this day forward, you are to be a partner in the firm of Malik Shoes. In consideration of your dedicated work over many years, and in recognition of our old friendship, I stipulate that the ownership of this company will be redrawn to give you an equal share. The business will henceforth be owned jointly between the two of us – Malik and Akeel.

Sincerely,
Karim Malik.

Ali had practically stopped breathing.

"But sir, is this true? Do you mean it?"

"Ali. Don't call me 'sir'. Call me Karim. I am your oldest friend, am I not?"

"Why yes," said Ali, his head spinning. "Of course, but…"

Karim knew what he was thinking. He had shown no love or friendship for years now. Had barely spoken to him. And sometimes when he did, crossly.

What had happened to make for this change?

He suddenly thought of the du'a that they had said the night before.

"Call on me, I will answer you." (Quran 40:60)

Ali looked across at Karim, whose face had broken out into a broad smile.

"Will you agree?" said Karim, grinning.

Ali choked back a sob. He was being presented with a gift of enormous value. The firm was worth a fortune. He would be rich.

But above all, he had his old friend back. He looked at Karim through eyes misting with tears, and he saw again the young boy with the pure heart – the boy of their youth.

"Karim, my friend," he cried. He stood and embraced him.

"Ali, my old friend. Forgive me."

Karim took Ali's hands and said,

"But what of Zain?"

"He is not well. I fear for him. The illness is bad, though Mariam says there is also hope. If only…"

"Ali, I promise that he will have the best doctors possible. I will spare no expense. You can do whatever it takes. I give you my word."

At this, Ali wept. His old friend was going to help save his son.

Karim stood and made the sign of prayer.

"I promise too that I will support Mariam's medical clinic, I will give money to Hajj Fawzi to help the orphans and I will pay for a new school."

Let us leave this tender scene now. You can imagine how much catching up they had to do, after so long.

Sometime after, the two men left the factory. Ali's first job as the new partner was to write a note to the workers for when they arrived.

On a large sheet of paper, he wrote a message in bold black letters and attached it to the door of the factory.

Malik Shoes is closed for the holy day of Eid. Spend it thanking the Lord for all we have.

"Let's make it three days," said Karim. "They deserve that."

Ali hugged Karim.

The sun was just about to rise.

From the mosque came the sound of people getting ready for the Eid Prayer.

People were coming out of their houses.

"Salaam," said Karim, grasping the hands of those he met. "Salaam. God is great."

Ali looked on in amazement.

This was a new Karim, thought Ali. A changed man. It truly was a miracle.

Karim was now handing out sweets, and saying, "Eid Mubarak – Blessed Eid."

A crowd had gathered outside the mosque.

"Hajj Fawzi!" called Karim. For he had spotted the man who ran the orphanage.

He whispered in the old man's ear.

Hajj Fawzi beamed with joy.

"In fact," said Karim in a soft voice, "let's open two orphanages!"

Hajj Fawzi hugged him. He had just saved all the abandoned children.

"God is great!"

"Shh."

But the old man could not contain himself.

Within seconds, word had got out.

"Malik is giving the funds for two orphanages!"

"It's amazing."

"It's a miracle!"

"Praise be to God."

They heard caller urging the worshippers to prayer.

Ahead of him, just climbing the steps to the mosque, were Ali's family.

Hanna and Jana were holding the hand of the little boy, Zain.

Karim looked at him anxiously. His face was pale, and he was walking slowly. But he was determined to offer a prayer for Eid.

"What are you doing here?" asked Karim, kneeling. "You should be resting at home, surely?" He looked to Hanna.

"But it is the best day of the year," said the boy. "God bless us, everyone."

"May I?" he asked the mother.

She nodded.

And Karim lifted the child onto his shoulders.

Hanna beckoned to Ali.

He told her the news.

She burst into tears.

"What happened last night? I can't believe the change in him."

"It was the du'a we said. *'Call on me. I will answer you.'* This is God's work."

The whole village had by now gathered at the mosque. The sun was just rising in the east.

Karim had put the boy down and was gently talking to him.

All around, news of Karim's change was spreading like a river of delight through the crowd.

"Imagine," said some. "He was cold. And now he is full of love."

"He is going to pay for all those poor children. It's the best news since the end of the war."

"He will save Zain, I know," said another.

They looked at Karim, with newfound admiration.

He had become, once more, a man of God.

Karim however suddenly looked up.

Someone had come into the mosque compound.

She had been working all night at the clinic. She looked tired.

"Karim?" she called out.

"Mariam."

He looked at her. She was just as beautiful as before. His heart melted with love.

She knew what had happened, without anyone telling her.

She smiled at him, a smile of happiness and indescribable pleasure.

Her words echoed in his head:

"I have every hope that he will one day change. And become again the man I loved."

"Mariam, I am back," he said.

She looked into his eyes. And she knew it was true.

Her beloved was back.

And they all went into the Mosque to give thanks and pray the prayer of Eid.

And so, our story ends.

But did Karim really change?

These were big promises. Did he honour them? Or did he go back to his old ways? Did he truly reform?

Well, I can assure you that he did more than he had promised.

Over the next few years Karim Malik became a father to every orphan.

He was a friend to all the downtrodden.

He had merely to hear of someone needing help, and he would provide it. With joy, and without the need for praise.

He went to mosque every day. And he prayed for guidance.

The factory flourished. Karim and Ali built a business that became the pride of all.

With his money, Karim turned Al Tawbah into the most beautiful village in the country.

Because of him, even the former enemies lived in peace and love in Al Tawbah.

And once again life was good, for everyone.

What of Karim himself, you wonder?

Well, I'm pleased to say that he married and had children. His love for his wife, always great, simply grew stronger. And she for him.

He grew older. And still he kept his word. He had changed forever.

And when he died, as a very old man, the whole village came to his funeral, to give thanks for his life. And all wept at losing such a wonderful loving man.

As Allah, the Almighty, in the Quran says,

"Let them pardon and forgive. Do you not love to be forgiven by Allah? And Allah is all-forgiving, most merciful." (Quran 24:22)

And so, concludes the life of my late loving husband, who transformed from darkness to light, in what became known as ...

The Miracle of Ramadan.

Mariam Malik

9 781922 583253